JOHN
BARRINGTON
COWLES

BY

SIR ARTHUR CONAN DOYLE

British Library Cataloguing-in-Publication Data
A catalogue record for this book is available from the
British Library

CONTENTS

SIR ARTHUR CONAN DOYLE

Arthur Conan Doyle was born in Edinburgh, Scotland, in 1859. It was between 1876 and 1881, while studying medicine at the University of Edinburgh, that he began writing short stories, and his first piece was published in *Chambers's Edinburgh Journal* before he was 20. In 1882, Conan Doyle opened an independent medical practice in Southsea, near Portsmouth. It was here, while waiting for patients, that he turned to writing fiction again, composing his first novel, *The Narrative of John Smith*.

In 1887, Conan Doyle's first significant work, *A Study in Scarlet*, appeared in *Beeton's Christmas Annual*. It featured the first appearance of detective Sherlock Holmes, the protagonist who was to eventually make Conan Doyle's reputation. A prolific writer, Conan Doyle continued to produce a range of fictional works over the following years. In 1893, feeling that the character of Sherlock Holmes was distracting him from his historical novels, he had Holmes apparently plunge to his death in the short story 'The Final Problem'. However, eight years later, following a public outcry from his readers, Conan Doyle 'resurrected' the detective in what is now widely regarded as his *magnum opus, The Hound of the Baskervilles*.

Sherlock Holmes went on to feature in fifty-six short stories and four novels, cementing Conan Doyle's reputation as probably the most famous crime writer of all time. Aside from his fiction, Conan Doyle was also a passionate political campaigner – a pamphlet he published in 1902, defending the United Kingdom's much-criticised role in the Boer War, is seen as a major contributor to his receiving of a knighthood in that same year.

In his later years, following the death of his son in World War I, Conan Doyle became deeply interested in spiritualism and psychic phenomena, producing several works on the subjects and engaging in a very public friendship and falling out with the American magician Harry Houdini. He died of a heart attack while living in East Sussex in 1930, aged 71.

JOHN BARRINGTON COWLES

It might seem rash of me to say that I ascribe the death of my poor friend, John Barrington Cowles, to any preternatural agency. I am aware that in the present state of public feeling a chain of evidence would require to be strong indeed before the possibility of such a conclusion could be admitted.

I shall therefore merely state the circumstances which led up to this sad event as concisely and as plainly as I can, and leave every reader to draw his own deductions. Perhaps there may be someone who can throw light upon what is dark to me.

I first met Barrington Cowles when I went up to Edinburgh University to take out medical classes there. My landlady in Northumberland Street had a large house, and, being a widow without children, she gained a livelihood by providing accommodation for several students.

Barrington Cowles happened to have taken a bedroom

upon the same floor as mine, and when we came to know each other better we shared a small sitting-room, in which we took our meals. In this manner we originated a friendship which was unmarred by the slightest disagreement up to the day of his death.

Cassel's Saturday Journal, 1886.

Cowles' father was the colonel of a Sikh regiment and had remained in India for many years. He allowed his son a handsome income, but seldom gave any other sign of parental affection—writing irregularly and briefly.

My friend, who had himself been born in India, and whose whole disposition was an ardent tropical one, was much hurt by this neglect. His mother was dead, and he had no other relation in the world to supply the blank.

Thus he came in time to concentrate all his affection upon me, and to confide in me in a manner which is rare among men. Even when a stronger and deeper passion came upon him, it never infringed upon the old tenderness between us. Cowles was a tall, slim young fellow, with an olive, Velasquez-like face, and dark, tender eyes. I have seldom seen a man who was more likely to excite a woman's interest, or to captivate her imagination. His expression was, as a rule, dreamy, and even languid; but if in conversation a subject arose which interested him he would be all animation in a moment. On such occasions his colour would heighten, his eyes gleam, and he could speak with an eloquence which would carry his audience with him.

In spite of these natural advantages he led a solitary life, avoiding female society, and reading with great diligence. He was one of the foremost men of his year, taking the senior medal for anatomy, and the Neil Arnott prize for physics.

How well I can recollect the first time we met her! Often and often I have recalled the circumstances, and tried to remember what the exact impression was which she produced on my mind at the time.

After we came to know her my judgment was warped, so that I am curious to recollect what my unbiassed (*sic*) instincts were. It is hard, however, to eliminate the feelings which reason or prejudice afterwards raised in me.

It was at the opening of the Royal Scottish Academy in the spring of 1879. My poor friend was passionately attached to art in every form, and a pleasing chord in music or a delicate effect upon canvas would give exquisite pleasure to his highly-strung nature. We had gone together to see the pictures, and were standing in the grand central salon, when I noticed an extremely beautiful woman standing at the other side of the room. In my whole life I have never seen such a classically perfect countenance. It was the real

Greek type—the forehead broad, very low, and as white as marble, with a cloudlet of delicate locks wreathing round it, the nose straight and clean cut, the lips inclined to thinness, the chin and lower jaw beautifully rounded off, and yet sufficiently developed to promise unusual strength of character. But those eyes—those wonderful eyes! If I could but give some faint idea of their varying moods, their steely hardness, their feminine softness, their power of command, their penetrating intensity suddenly melting away into an expression of womanly weakness—but I am speaking now of future impressions!

There was a tall, yellow-haired young man with this lady, whom I at once recognised as a law student with whom I had a slight acquaintance.

Archibald Reeves—for that was his name—was a dashing, handsome young fellow, and had at one time been a ringleader in every university escapade; but of late I had seen little of him, and the report was that he was engaged to be married. His companion was, then, I presumed, his fiancée. I seated myself upon the velvet settee in the centre of the room, and furtively watched the couple from behind my catalogue.

The more I looked at her the more her beauty grew upon me. She was somewhat short in stature, it is true; but her figure was perfection, and she bore herself in such a fashion that it was only by actual comparison that one would have known her to be under the medium height. As I kept my eyes upon them, Reeves was called away for some reason, and the young lady was left alone. Turning her back to the pictures, she passed the time until the return of her escort in taking a deliberate survey of the company, without paying the least heed to the fact that a dozen pair of eyes, attracted by her elegance and beauty, were bent curiously upon her. With one of her hands holding the red silk cord which railed off the pictures, she stood languidly moving her eyes from face to face with as little self-consciousness as if she were looking at the canvas creatures behind her. Suddenly, as I watched her, I saw her gaze become fixed, and, as it were, intense. I followed the direction of her looks, wondering what could have attracted her so strongly.

John Barrington Cowles was standing before a picture— one, I think, by Noel Paton—I know that the subject was a noble and ethereal one. His profile was turned toward us, and never have I seen him to such advantage. I have said that he was a strikingly handsome man, but at that moment he looked absolutely magnificent. It was evident that he had momentarily forgotten his surroundings, and that his whole soul was in sympathy with the picture before him. His eyes sparkled, and a dusky pink shone through his clear olive cheeks. She continued to watch him fixedly, with a look of interest upon her face, until he came out of his reverie with a start, and turned abruptly round, so that his gaze met hers. She glanced away at once, but his eyes remained fixed upon her for some moments. The picture was forgotten already, and his soul had come down to earth once more.

We caught sight of her once or twice before we left, and each time I noticed my friend look after her. He made no remark, however, until we got out into the open air, and were walking arm-in-arm along Princes Street.

"Did you notice that beautiful woman, in the dark dress, with the white fur?" he asked.

"Yes, I saw her," I answered.

"Do you know her?" he asked eagerly. "Have you any idea who she is?"

"I don't know her personally," I replied. "But I have no doubt I could find out all about her, for I believe she is engaged to young Archie Reeves, and he and I have a lot of mutual friends."

"Engaged!" ejaculated Cowles.

"Why, my dear boy," I said, laughing, "you don't mean to say you are so susceptible that the fact that a girl to whom you never spoke in your life is engaged is enough to upset you?"

"Well, not exactly to upset me," he answered, forcing a laugh. "But I don't mind telling you, Armitage, that I never was so taken by any one in my life. It wasn't the mere beauty of the face—though that was perfect enough—but it was the character and the intellect upon it. I hope, if she is engaged, that it is to some man who will be worthy of her."

"Why," I remarked, "you speak quite feelingly. It is a clear case of love at first sight, Jack. However, to put your perturbed spirit at rest, I'll make a point of finding out all about her whenever I meet any fellow who is likely to know."

Barrington Cowles thanked me, and the conversation drifted off into other channels. For several days neither of us made any allusion to the subject, though my companion was perhaps a little more dreamy and distraught than usual. The incident had almost vanished from my remembrance, when one day young Brodie, who is a second cousin of mine, came up to me on the university steps with the face of a bearer of tidings.

"I say," he began, "you know Reeves, don't you?"

"Yes. What of him?"

"His engagement is off."

"Off!" I cried. "Why, I only learned the other day that it was on."

"Oh, yes—it's all off. His brother told me so. Deucedly mean of Reeves, you know, if he has backed out of it, for she was an uncommonly nice girl."

"I've seen her," I said, "but I don't know her name."

"She is a Miss Northcott, and lives with an old aunt of

hers in Abercrombie Place. Nobody knows anything about her people, or where she comes from. Anyhow, she is about the most unlucky girl in the world, poor soul!"

"Why unlucky?"

"Well, you know, this was her second engagement," said young Brodie, who had a marvellous knack of knowing everything about everybody. "She was engaged to Prescott—William Prescott, who died. That was a very sad affair. The wedding day was fixed, and the whole thing looked as straight as a die when the smash came."

"What smash?" I asked, with some dim recollection of the circumstances.

"Why, Prescott's death. He came to Abercrombie Place one night, and stayed very late. No one knows exactly when he left, but about one in the morning a fellow who knew him met him walking rapidly in the direction of the Queen's Park. He bade him good night, but Prescott hurried on without heeding him, and that was the last time he was ever seen alive. Three days afterwards his body was found floating in St. Margaret's Loch, under St. Anthony's Chapel. No one could ever understand it, but of course the verdict brought it in as temporary insanity."

"It was very strange," I remarked.

"Yes, and deucedly rough on the poor girl," said Brodie. "Now that this other blow has come it will quite crush her.

So gentle and ladylike she is too!"

"You know her personally, then!" I asked.

"Oh, yes, I know her. I have met her several times. I could easily manage that you should be introduced to her."

"Well," I answered, "it's not so much for my own sake as for a friend of mine. However, I don't suppose she will go out much for some little time after this. When she does I will take advantage of your offer."

We shook hands on this, and I thought no more of the matter for some time.

The next incident which I have to relate as bearing at all upon the question of Miss Northcott is an unpleasant one. Yet I must detail it as accurately as possible, since it may throw some light upon the sequel. One cold night, several months after the conversation with my second cousin which I have quoted above, I was walking down one of the lowest streets in the city on my way back from a case which I had been attending. It was very late, and I was picking my way among the dirty loungers who were clustering round the doors of a great gin-palace, when a man staggered out from among them, and held out his hand to me with a drunken leer. The gaslight fell full upon his face, and, to my intense astonishment, I recognised in the degraded creature before me my former acquaintance, young Archibald Reeves, who had once been famous as one of the most dressy and particular men in the whole college. I was so utterly surprised that for a moment I almost doubted the evidence of my own senses; but there was no mistaking those features, which, though bloated with drink, still retained something of their former comeliness. I was determined to rescue him, for one night at least, from the company into which he had fallen.

"Holloa, Reeves!" I said. "Come along with me. I'm going in your direction."

He muttered some incoherent apology for his condition, and took my arm. As I supported him toward his lodgings I could see that he was not only suffering from the effects of a recent debauch, but that a long course of intemperance had affected his nerves and his brain. His hand when I touched it was dry and feverish, and he started from every shadow which fell upon the pavement. He rambled in his speech, too, in a manner which suggested the delirium of disease rather than the talk of a drunkard.

When I got him to his lodgings I partially undressed him and laid him upon his bed. His pulse at this time was very high, and he was evidently extremely feverish. He seemed to have sunk into a doze; and I was about to steal out of the room to warn his landlady of his condition, when he started up and caught me by the sleeve of my coat.

"Don't go!" he cried. "I feel better when you are here. I am safe from her then."

"From her!" I said. "From whom?"

"Her! her!" he answered peevishly. "Ah! you don't know her. She is the devil! Beautiful—beautiful; but the devil!"

"You are feverish and excited," I said. "Try and get a little sleep. You will wake better."

"Sleep!" he groaned. "How am I to sleep when I see her sitting down yonder at the foot of the bed with her great eyes watching and watching hour after hour? I tell you it saps all the strength and manhood out of me. That's what makes me drink. God help me—I'm half drunk now!"

"You are very ill," I said, putting some vinegar to his temples; "and you are delirious. You don't know what you say."

"Yes, I do," he interrupted sharply, looking up at me. "I know very well what I say. I brought it upon myself. It is my own choice. But I couldn't—no, by heaven, I couldn't— accept the alternative. I couldn't keep my faith to her. It was more than man could do."

I sat by the side of the bed, holding one of his burning hands in mine, and wondering over his strange words. He lay still for some time, and then, raising his eyes to me, said in a most plaintive voice—

"Why did she not give me warning sooner? Why did she wait until I had learned to love her so?"

He repeated this question several times, rolling his feverish head from side to side, and then he dropped into a troubled sleep. I crept out of the room, and, having seen that he would be properly cared for, left the house. His words, however, rang in my ears for days afterwards, and assumed a deeper significance when taken with what was to come.

My friend, Barrington Cowles, had been away for his summer holidays, and I had heard nothing of him for several months. When the winter session came on, however, I received a telegram from him, asking me to secure the old rooms in Northumberland Street for him, and telling me the train by which he would arrive. I went down to meet him, and was delighted to find him looking wonderfully hearty and well.

"By the way," he said suddenly, that night, as we sat in our chairs by the fire, talking over the events of the holidays, "you have never congratulated me yet!"

"On what, my boy?" I asked.

"What! Do you mean to say you have not heard of my engagement?"

"Engagement! No!" I answered. "However, I am delighted to hear it, and congratulate you with all my heart."

"I wonder it didn't come to your ears," he said. "It was the queerest thing. You remember that girl whom we both admired so much at the Academy?"

"What!" I cried, with a vague feeling of apprehension at my heart. "You don't mean to say that you are engaged to her?"

"I thought you would be surprised," he answered. "When I was staying with an old aunt of mine in Peterhead, in Aberdeenshire, the Northcotts happened to come there on a visit, and as we had mutual friends we soon met. I found out that it was a false alarm about her being engaged, and then—well, you know what it is when you are thrown into the society of such a girl in a place like Peterhead. Not, mind you," he added, "that I consider I did a foolish or hasty thing. I have never regretted it for a moment. The more I know Kate the more I admire her and love her. However, you must be introduced to her, and then you will form your own opinion."

I expressed my pleasure at the prospect, and endeavoured to speak as lightly as I could to Cowles upon the subject, but I felt depressed and anxious at heart. The words of Reeves and the unhappy fate of young Prescott recurred to my recollection, and though I could assign no tangible reason for it, a vague, dim fear and distrust of the woman took possession of me. It may be that this was foolish prejudice and superstition upon my part, and that I involuntarily contorted her future doings and sayings to fit into some half-formed wild theory of my own. This has been suggested to me by others as an explanation of my narrative. They are welcome to their opinion if they can reconcile it with the facts which I have to tell.

I went round with my friend a few days afterwards to call upon Miss Northcott. I remember that, as we went down Abercrombie Place, our attention was attracted by the shrill yelping of a dog—which noise proved eventually to come from the house to which we were bound. We were shown upstairs, where I was introduced to old Mrs. Merton, Miss Northcott's aunt, and to the young lady herself. She looked as beautiful as ever, and I could not wonder at my friend's infatuation. Her face was a little more flushed than usual, and she held in her hand a heavy dog-whip, with which she had been chastising a small Scotch terrier, whose cries we had heard in the street. The poor brute was cringing up against the wall, whining piteously, and evidently completely cowed.

"So Kate," said my friend, after we had taken our seats, "you have been falling out with Carlo again."

"Only a very little quarrel this time," she said, smiling charmingly. "He is a dear, good old fellow, but he needs correction now and then." Then, turning to me, "We all do that, Mr. Armitage, don't we? What a capital thing if, instead of receiving a collective punishment at the end of our lives, we were to have one at once, as the dogs do, when we did anything wicked. It would make us more careful, wouldn't it?"

I acknowledged that it would.

"Supposing that every time a man misbehaved himself a gigantic hand were to seize him, and he were lashed with a whip until he fainted"—she clenched her white fingers as she spoke, and cut out viciously with the dog-whip—"it would do more to keep him good than any number of high-minded theories of morality."

"Why, Kate," said my friend, "you are quite savage today."

"No, Jack," she laughed. "I'm only propounding a theory for Mr. Armitage's consideration."

The two began to chat together about some Aberdeenshire reminiscence, and I had time to observe Mrs. Merton, who had remained silent during our short conversation. She was a very strange-looking old lady. What attracted attention most in her appearance was the utter want of colour which she exhibited. Her hair was snow-white, and her face extremely pale. Her lips were bloodless, and even her eyes were of such a light tinge of blue that they hardly relieved the general pallor. Her dress was a gray silk, which harmonised with her general appearance. She had a peculiar expression of countenance, which I was unable at the moment to refer to its proper cause.

She was working at some old-fashioned piece of ornamental needlework, and as she moved her arms her dress gave forth a dry, melancholy rustling, like the sound of leaves in the autumn. There was something mournful and depressing in the sight of her. I moved my chair a little nearer, and asked her how she liked Edinburgh, and whether she had been there long. When I spoke to her she started and looked up at me with a scared look on her face. Then I saw in a moment what the expression was which I had observed there. It was one of fear—intense and overpowering fear. It was so marked that I could have staked my life on the woman before me having at some period of her life been subjected to some terrible experience or dreadful misfortune.

"Oh, yes, I like it," she said, in a soft, timid voice, "and we have been here long—that is, not very long. We move about a great deal." She spoke with hesitation, as if afraid of committing herself.

"You are a native of Scotland, I presume?" I said. "No—that is, not entirely. We are not natives of any place. We are cosmopolitan, you know." She glanced round in the direction of Miss Northcott as she spoke, but the two were still chatting together near the window. Then she suddenly bent forward to me, with a look of intense earnestness upon her face, and said—

"Don't talk to me any more, please. She does not like it, and I shall suffer for it afterwards. Please, don't do it."

I was about to ask her the reason for this strange request, but when she saw I was going to address her, she rose and walked slowly out of the room. As she did so I perceived that the lovers had ceased to talk and that Miss Northcott was looking at me with her keen, gray eyes.

"You must excuse my aunt, Mr. Armitage," she said, "she is odd, and easily fatigued. Come over and look at my album."

We spent some time examining the portraits. Miss Northcott's father and mother were apparently ordinary mortals enough, and I could not detect in either of them any traces of the character which showed itself in their daughter's face. There was one old daguerreotype, however, which arrested my attention. It represented a man of about the age of forty, and strikingly handsome. He was clean shaven, and extraordinary power was expressed upon his prominent lower jaw and firm, straight mouth. His eyes were somewhat deeply set in his head, however, and there was a snake-like flattening at the upper part of his forehead, which detracted from his appearance. I almost involuntarily, when I saw the head, pointed to it, and exclaimed—

"There is your prototype in your family, Miss Northcott."

"Do you think so?" she said. "I am afraid you are paying me a very bad compliment. Uncle Anthony was always considered the black sheep of the family."

"Indeed," I answered. "My remark was an unfortunate one, then."

"Oh, don't mind that," she said. "I always thought myself that he was worth all of them put together. He was an officer in the Forty-first Regiment, and he was killed in action during the Persian War—so he died nobly, at any rate."

"That's the sort of death I should like to die," said Cowles, his dark eyes flashing, as they would when he was excited. "I often wish I had taken to my father's profession instead of this vile pill-compounding drudgery."

"Come, Jack, you are not going to die any sort of death yet," she said, tenderly taking his hand in hers.

I could not understand the woman. There was such an extraordinary mixture of masculine decision and womanly tenderness about her, with the consciousness of something all her own in the background, that she fairly puzzled me. I hardly knew, therefore, how to answer Cowles when, as we walked down the street together, he asked the comprehensive question—

"Well, what do you think of her?"

"I think she is wonderfully beautiful," I

answered guardedly.

"That, of course," he replied irritably. "You knew that before you came!"

"I think she is very clever too," I remarked.

Barrington Cowles walked on for some time, and then he suddenly turned on me with the strange question—

"Do you think she is cruel? Do you think she is the sort of girl who would take a pleasure in inflicting pain?"

"Well, really," I answered, "I have hardly had time to form an opinion."

We then walked on for some time in silence.

"She is an old fool," at length muttered Cowles. "She is mad."

"Who is?" I asked.

"Why, that old woman—that aunt of Kate's—Mrs. Merton, or whatever her name is."

Then I knew that my poor colourless friend had been speaking to Cowles, but he never said anything more as to the nature of her communication.

My companion went to bed early that night, and I sat up a long time by the fire, thinking over all that I had seen and heard. I felt that there was some mystery about the girl— some dark fatality so strange as to defy conjecture. I thought of Prescott's interview with her before their marriage, and the fatal termination of it. I coupled it with poor drunken

Reeves' plaintive cry, "Why did she not tell me sooner?" and with the other words he had spoken. Then my mind ran over Mrs. Merton's warning to me, Cowles' reference to her, and even the episode of the whip and the cringing dog.

The whole effect of my recollections was unpleasant to a degree, and yet there was no tangible charge which I could bring against the woman. It would be worse than useless to attempt to warn my friend until I had definitely made up my mind what I was to warn him against. He would treat any charge against her with scorn. What could I do? How could I get at some tangible conclusion as to her character and antecedents? No one in Edinburgh knew them except as recent acquaintances. She was an orphan, and as far as I knew she had never disclosed where her former home had been. Suddenly an idea struck me. Among my father's friends there was a Colonel Joyce, who had served a long time in India upon the staff, and who would be likely to know most of the officers who had been out there since the Mutiny. I sat down at once, and, having trimmed the lamp, proceeded to write a letter to the Colonel. I told him that I was very curious to gain some particulars about a certain Captain Northcott, who had served in the Forty-first Foot, and who had fallen in the Persian War. I described the man as well as I could from my recollection of the daguerreotype, and then, having directed the letter, posted it that very night, after which, feeling that I had done all that could be done, I retired to bed, with a mind too anxious to allow me to sleep.

PART II

I got an answer from Leicester, where the Colonel resided, within two days. I have it before me as I write, and copy it verbatim.

"DEAR BOB" [it said] *"I remember the man well. I was with him at Calcutta, and afterwards at Hyderabad. He was a curious, solitary sort of mortal; but a gallant soldier enough, for he distinguished himself at Sobraon, and was wounded, if I remember right. He was not popular in his corps—they said he was a pitiless, cold-blooded fellow, with no geniality in him. There was a rumour, too, that he was a devil-worshipper, or something of that sort, and also that he had the evil eye, which, of course, was all nonsense. He had some strange theories, I remember, about the power of the human will and the effects of mind upon matter.*

"How are you getting on with your medical studies? Never forget, my boy, that your father's son has every claim upon me, and that if I can serve you in any way I am always at your command.—Ever affectionately yours, EDWARD JOYCE.

"P.S.—By the way, Northcott did not fall in action. He was killed after peace was declared in a crazy attempt to get some of the eternal fire from the sun-worshippers' temple. There was considerable mystery about his death."

I read this epistle over several times—at first with a feeling of satisfaction, and then with one of disappointment. I had come on some curious information, and yet hardly what I wanted. He was an eccentric man, a devil-worshipper, and rumoured to have the power of the evil eye. I could believe the young lady's eyes, when endowed with that cold, gray shimmer which I had noticed in them once or twice, to be capable of any evil which human eye ever wrought; but still the superstition was an effete one. Was there not more meaning in that sentence which followed—"He had theories of the power of the human will and of the effect of mind upon matter"? I remember having once read a quaint treatise, which I had imagined to be mere charlatanism at the time, of the power of certain human minds, and of effects produced by them at a distance.

Was Miss Northcott endowed with some exceptional power of the sort?

The idea grew upon me, and very shortly I had evidence which convinced me of the truth of the supposition.

It happened that at the very time when my mind was dwelling upon this subject, I saw a notice in the paper that our town was to be visited by Dr. Messinger, the well-known medium and mesmerist. Messinger was a man whose performance, such as it was, had been again and again pronounced to be genuine by competent judges. He was far above trickery, and had the reputation of being the soundest living authority upon the strange pseudo-sciences of animal magnetism and electro-biology. Determined, therefore, to see what the human will could do, even against all the disadvantages of glaring footlights and a public platform, I took a ticket for the first night of the performance, and went with several student friends.

We had secured one of the side boxes, and did not arrive until after the performance had begun. I had hardly taken my seat before I recognised Barrington Cowles, with his fiancee and old Mrs. Merton, sitting in the third or fourth row of the stalls. They caught sight of me at almost the same moment, and we bowed to each other. The first portion of the lecture was somewhat commonplace, the lecturer giving tricks of pure legerdemain, with one or two manifestations of mesmerism, performed upon a subject whom he had brought with him. He gave us an exhibition of clairvoyance too, throwing his subject into a trance, and then demanding particulars as to the movements of absent friends, and the whereabouts of hidden objects all of which appeared to be answered satisfactorily. I had seen all this before, however. What I wanted to see now was the effect of the lecturer's will when exerted upon some independent member of the audience.

He came round to that as the concluding exhibition in his

performance. "I have shown you," he said, "that a mesmerised subject is entirely dominated by the will of the mesmeriser. He loses all power of volition, and his very thoughts are such as are suggested to him by the master-mind. The same end may be attained without any preliminary process. A strong will can, simply by virtue of its strength, take possession of a weaker one, even at a distance, and can regulate the impulses and the actions of the owner of it. If there was one man in the world who had a very much more highly-developed will than any of the rest of the human family, there is no reason why he should not be able to rule over them all, and to reduce his fellow-creatures to the condition of automatons. Happily there is such a dead level of mental power, or rather of mental weakness, among us that such a catastrophe is not likely to occur; but still within our small compass there are variations which produce surprising effects. I shall now single out one of the audience, and endeavour 'by the mere power of will' to compel him to come upon the platform, and do and say what I wish. Let me assure you that there is no collusion, and that the subject whom I may select is at perfect liberty to resent to the uttermost any impulse which I may communicate to him."

With these words the lecturer came to the front of the platform, and glanced over the first few rows of the stalls. No doubt Cowles' dark skin and bright eyes marked him out as a man of a highly nervous temperament, for the mesmerist picked him out in a moment, and fixed his eyes upon him. I saw my friend give a start of surprise, and then settle down in his chair, as if to express his determination not to yield to the influence of the operator. Messinger was not a man whose head denoted any great brain-power, but his gaze was singularly intense and penetrating. Under the influence of it Cowles made one or two spasmodic motions of his hands, as if to grasp the sides of his seat, and then half rose, but only to sink down again, though with an evident effort. I was watching the scene with intense interest, when I happened to catch a glimpse of Miss Northcott's face. She was sitting with her eyes fixed intently upon the mesmerist, and with such an expression of concentrated power upon her features as I have never seen on any other human countenance. Her jaw was firmly set, her lips compressed, and her face as hard as if it were a beautiful sculpture cut out of the whitest marble. Her eyebrows were drawn down, however, and from beneath them her gray eyes seemed to sparkle and gleam with a cold light. I looked at Cowles again, expecting every moment to see him rise and obey the mesmerist's wishes, when there came from the platform a short, gasping cry as of a man utterly worn out and prostrated by a prolonged struggle. Messinger was leaning against the table, his hand to his forehead, and the perspiration pouring down his face.

"I won't go on," he cried, addressing the audience. "There is a stronger will than mine acting against me. You must excuse me for tonight." The man was evidently ill, and utterly unable to proceed, so the curtain was lowered, and the audience dispersed, with many comments upon the lecturer's sudden indisposition.

I waited outside the hall until my friend and the ladies came out. Cowles was laughing over his recent experience.

"He didn't succeed with me, Bob," he cried triumphantly, as he shook my hand. "I think he caught a Tartar that time."

"Yes," said Miss Northcott, "I think that Jack ought to be very proud of his strength of mind; don't you! Mr. Armitage?"

"It took me all my time, though," my friend said seriously. "You can't conceive what a strange feeling I had once or twice. All the strength seemed to have gone out of me—especially just before he collapsed himself."

I walked round with Cowles in order to see the ladies home. He walked in front with Mrs. Merton, and I found myself behind with the young lady. For a minute or so I walked beside her without making any remark, and then I suddenly blurted out, in a manner which must have seemed somewhat brusque to her—

"You did that, Miss Northcott."

"Did what?" she asked sharply.

"Why, mesmerised the mesmeriser—I suppose that is the best way of describing the transaction."

"What a strange idea!" she said, laughing. "You give me credit for a strong will then?"

"Yes," I said. "For a dangerously strong one."

"Why dangerous?" she asked, in a tone of surprise.

"I think," I answered, "that any will which can exercise such power is dangerous—for there is always a chance of its being turned to bad uses."

"You would make me out a very dreadful individual, Mr. Armitage," she said; and then looking up suddenly in my face—"You have never liked me. You are suspicious of me and distrust me, though I have never given you cause."

The accusation was so sudden and so true that I was unable to find any reply to it. She paused for a moment, and then said in a voice which was hard and cold—

"Don't let your prejudice lead you to interfere with me, however, or say anything to your friend, Mr. Cowles, which might lead to a difference between us. You would find that to be very bad policy."

There was something in the way she spoke which gave an indescribable air of a threat to these few words.

"I have no power," I said, "to interfere with your plans for the future. I cannot help, however, from what I have seen and heard, having fears for my friend."

"Fears!" she repeated scornfully. "Pray what have you seen and heard. Something from Mr. Reeves, perhaps—I believe he is another of your friends?"

"He never mentioned your name to me," I answered, truthfully enough. "You will be sorry to hear that he is dying." As I said it we passed by a lighted window, and I glanced down to see what effect my words had upon her. She was laughing—there was no doubt of it; she was laughing quietly to herself. I could see merriment in every feature of her face. I feared and mistrusted the woman from that moment more than ever.

We said little more that night. When we parted she gave me a quick, warning glance, as if to remind me of what she had said about the danger of interference. Her cautions would have made little difference to me could I have seen my way to benefiting Barrington Cowles by anything which I might say. But what could I say? I might say that her former suitors had been unfortunate. I might say that I believed her to be a cruel-hearted woman. I might say that I considered her to possess wonderful, and almost preternatural powers. What impression would any of these accusations make upon an ardent lover—a man with my friend's enthusiastic temperament? I felt that it would be useless to advance them, so I was silent.

31

And now I come to the beginning of the end. Hitherto much has been surmise and inference and hearsay. It is my painful task to relate now, as dispassionately and as accurately as I can, what actually occurred under my own notice, and to reduce to writing the events which preceded the death of my friend.

Toward the end of the winter Cowles remarked to me that he intended to marry Miss Northcott as soon as possible—probably some time in the spring. He was, as I have already remarked, fairly well off, and the young lady had some money of her own, so that there was no pecuniary reason for a long engagement. "We are going to take a little house out at Corstorphine," he said, "and we hope to see your face at our table, Bob, as often as you can possibly come." I thanked him, and tried to shake off my apprehensions, and persuade myself that all would yet be well.

It was about three weeks before the time fixed for the marriage, that Cowles remarked to me one evening that he feared he would be late that night. "I have had a note from Kate," he said, "asking me to call about eleven o'clock tonight, which seems rather a late hour, but perhaps she wants to talk over something quietly after old Mrs. Merton retires."

It was not until after my friend's departure that I suddenly recollected the mysterious interview which I had been told of as preceding the suicide of young Prescott. Then I thought of the ravings of poor Reeves, rendered more tragic by the fact that I had heard that very day of his death. What was the meaning of it all? Had this woman some baleful secret to disclose which must be known before her marriage? Was it some reason which forbade her to marry? Or was it some reason which forbade others to marry her? I felt so uneasy that I would have followed Cowles, even at the risk of offending him, and endeavoured to dissuade him from keeping his appointment, but a glance at the clock showed me that I was too late.

I was determined to wait up for his return, so I piled some coals upon the fire and took down a novel from the shelf. My thoughts proved more interesting than the book, however, and I threw it on one side. An indefinable feeling of anxiety and depression weighed upon me. Twelve o'clock came, and then half-past, without any sign of my friend. It was nearly one when I heard a step in the street outside, and then a knocking at the door. I was surprised, as I knew that my friend always carried a key—however, I hurried down and undid the latch. As the door flew open I knew in a moment that my worst apprehensions had been fulfilled. Barrington Cowles was leaning against the railings outside with his face sunk upon his breast, and his whole attitude expressive of the most intense despondency. As he passed in he gave a stagger, and would have fallen had I not thrown my left arm around him. Supporting him with this, and holding the lamp in my other hand, I led him slowly upstairs into our sitting-room. He sank down upon the sofa without a word. Now that I could get a good view of him, I was horrified to see the change which had come over him. His face was deadly pale, and his very lips were bloodless. His cheeks and forehead were clammy, his eyes glazed, and his whole expression altered. He looked like a man who had gone through some terrible ordeal, and was thoroughly unnerved.

"My dear fellow, what is the matter?" I asked, breaking the silence. "Nothing amiss, I trust? Are you unwell?"

"Brandy!" he gasped. "Give me some brandy!"

I took out the decanter, and was about to help him, when he snatched it from me with a trembling hand, and poured out nearly half a tumbler of the spirit. He was usually a most abstemious man, but he took this off at a gulp without adding any water to it.

It seemed to do him good, for the colour began to come back to his face, and he leaned upon his elbow.

"My engagement is off, Bob," he said, trying to speak calmly, but with a tremor in his voice which he could not conceal. "It is all over."

"Cheer up!" I answered, trying to encourage him. Don't get down on your luck. How was it? What was it all about?"

"About?" he groaned, covering his face with his hands. "If I did tell you, Bob, you would not believe it. It is too dreadful—too horrible—unutterably awful and incredible! O Kate, Kate!" and he rocked himself to and fro in his grief; "I pictured you an angel and I find you a—"

"A what?" I asked, for he had paused.

He looked at me with a vacant stare, and then suddenly burst out, waving his arms: "A fiend!" he cried. "A ghoul from the pit! A vampire soul behind a lovely face! Now, God forgive me!" he went on in a lower tone, turning his face to the wall. "I have said more than I should. I have loved her too much to speak of her as she is. I love her too much now."

He lay still for some time, and I had hoped that the brandy had had the effect of sending him to sleep, when he suddenly turned his face toward me.

"Did you ever read of wehr-wolves?" he asked.

I answered that I had.

"There is a story," he said thoughtfully, "in one of Marryat's books, about a beautiful woman who took the form of a wolf at night and devoured her own children. I wonder what put that idea into Marryat's head?"

He pondered for some minutes, and then he cried out for some more brandy. There was a small bottle of laudanum upon the table, and I managed, by insisting upon helping him myself, to mix about half a drachm with the spirits. He drank it off, and sank his head once more upon the pillow. "Anything better than that," he groaned. "Death is better than that. Crime and cruelty; cruelty and crime. Anything is better than that," and so on, with the monotonous refrain, until at last the words became indistinct, his eyelids closed over his weary eyes, and he sank into a profound slumber. I carried him into his bedroom without arousing him; and making a couch for myself out of the chairs, I remained by his side all night.

In the morning Barrington Cowles was in a high fever. For weeks he lingered between life and death. The highest medical skill of Edinburgh was called in, and his vigorous constitution slowly got the better of his disease. I nursed him during this anxious time; but through all his wild delirium and ravings he never let a word escape him which explained the mystery connected with Miss Northcott. Sometimes he spoke of her in the tenderest words and most loving voice. At others he screamed out that she was a fiend, and stretched out his arms, as if to keep her off. Several times he cried that he would not sell his soul for a beautiful face, and then he would moan in a most piteous voice, "But I love her—I love her for all that; I shall never cease to love her."

When he came to himself he was an altered man. His severe illness had emaciated him greatly, but his dark eyes had lost none of their brightness. They shone out with startling brilliancy from under his dark, overhanging brows. His manner was eccentric and variable—sometimes irritable, sometimes recklessly mirthful, but never natural. He would glance about him in a strange, suspicious manner, like one who feared something, and yet hardly knew what it was he dreaded. He never mentioned Miss Northcott's name—never until that fatal evening of which I have now to speak.

In an endeavour to break the current of his thoughts by frequent change of scene, I travelled with him through the highlands of Scotland, and afterwards down the east coast. In one of these peregrinations of ours we visited the Isle of May, an island near the mouth of the Firth of Forth, which, except in the tourist season, is singularly barren and desolate. Beyond the keeper of the lighthouse there are only one or two families of poor fisherfolk, who sustain a precarious existence by their nets, and by the capture of cormorants and solan geese. This grim spot seemed to have such a fascination for Cowles that we engaged a room in one of the fishermen's huts, with the intention of passing a week or two there. I found it very dull, but the loneliness appeared to be a relief to my friend's mind. He lost the look of apprehension which had become habitual to him, and became something like his old self.

He would wander round the island all day, looking down

from the summit of the great cliffs which gird it round, and watching the long green waves as they came booming in and burst in a shower of spray over the rocks beneath.

One night—I think it was our third or fourth on the island—Barrington Cowles and I went outside the cottage before retiring to rest, to enjoy a little fresh air, for our room was small, and the rough lamp caused an unpleasant odour. How well I remember every little circumstance in connection with that night! It promised to be tempestuous, for the clouds were piling up in the north-west, and the dark wrack was drifting across the face of the moon, throwing alternate belts of light and shade upon the rugged surface of the island and the restless sea beyond.

We were standing talking close by the door of the cottage, and I was thinking to myself that my friend was more cheerful than he had been since his illness, when he gave a sudden, sharp cry, and looking round at him I saw, by the light of the moon, an expression of unutterable horror come over his features. His eyes became fixed and staring, as if riveted upon some approaching object, and he extended his long thin forefinger, which quivered as he pointed.

"Look there!" he cried. "It is she! It is she! You see her there coming down the side of the brae." He gripped me convulsively by the wrist as he spoke. "There she is, coming toward us!"

"Who?" I cried, straining my eyes into the darkness.

"She—Kate—Kate Northcott!" he screamed. "She has come for me. Hold me fast, old friend. Don't let me go!"

"Hold up, old man," I said, clapping him on the shoulder. "Pull yourself together; you are dreaming; there is nothing to fear."

"She is gone!" he cried, with a gasp of relief. "No, by heaven! there she is again, and nearer—coming nearer. She told me she would come for me, and she keeps her word."

"Come into the house," I said. His hand, as I grasped it, was as cold as ice.

"Ah, I knew it!" he shouted. "There she is, waving her arms. She is beckoning to me. It is the signal. I must go. I am coming, Kate; I am coming!"

I threw my arms around him, but he burst from me with superhuman strength, and dashed into the darkness of the night. I followed him, calling to him to stop, but he ran the more swiftly. When the moon shone out between the clouds I could catch a glimpse of his dark figure, running rapidly in a straight line, as if to reach some definite goal. It may have been imagination, but it seemed to me that in the flickering light I could distinguish a vague something in front of him—a shimmering form which eluded his grasp and led him onwards. I saw his outlines stand out hard against the sky behind him as he surmounted the brow of a little hill, then he disappeared, and that was the last ever seen by mortal eye of Barrington Cowles.

The fishermen and I walked round the island all that night with lanterns, and examined every nook and corner without seeing a trace of my poor lost friend. The direction in which he had been running terminated in a rugged line of jagged cliffs overhanging the sea. At one place here the edge was somewhat crumbled, and there appeared marks upon the turf which might have been left by human feet. We lay upon our faces at this spot, and peered with our lanterns over the edge, looking down on the boiling surge two hundred feet below. As we lay there, suddenly, above the beating of the waves and the howling of the wind, there rose a strange wild screech from the abyss below. The fishermen—a naturally superstitious race—averred that it was the sound of a woman's laughter, and I could hardly persuade them to continue the search. For my own part I think it may have been the cry of some sea-fowl startled from its nest by the flash of the lantern. However that may be, I never wish to hear such a sound again.

And now I have come to the end of the painful duty which I have undertaken. I have told as plainly and as accurately as I could the story of the death of John Barrington Cowles, and the train of events which preceded it. I am aware that to others the sad episode seemed commonplace enough. Here is the prosaic account which appeared in the Scotsman a couple of days afterwards:—"Sad Occurrence on the Isle of May.—The Isle of May has been the scene of a sad disaster. Mr. John Barrington Cowles, a gentleman well known in University circles as a most distinguished student, and the present holder of the Neil Arnott prize for physics, has been recruiting his health in this quiet retreat. The night before last he suddenly left his friend, Mr. Robert Armitage, and he has not since been heard of. It is almost certain that he has met his death by falling over the cliffs which surround the island. Mr. Cowles' health has been failing for some time, partly from over study and partly from worry connected with family affairs. By his death the University loses one of her most promising alumni."

I have nothing more to add to my statement. I have unburdened my mind of all that I know. I can well conceive that many, after weighing all that I have said, will see no ground for an accusation against Miss Northcott. They will say that, because a man of a naturally excitable disposition says and does wild things, and even eventually commits self-murder after a sudden and heavy disappointment, there is no reason why vague charges should be advanced against a young lady. To this, I answer that they are welcome to their opinion. For my own part, I ascribe the death of William Prescott, of Archibald Reeves, and of John Barrington

Cowles to this woman with as much confidence as if I had seen her drive a dagger into their hearts.

You ask me, no doubt, what my own theory is which will explain all these strange facts. I have none, or, at best, a dim and vague one. That Miss Northcott possessed extraordinary powers over the minds, and through the minds over the bodies, of others, I am convinced, as well as that her instincts were to use this power for base and cruel purposes. That some even more fiendish and terrible phase of character lay behind this—some horrible trait which it was necessary for her to reveal before marriage—is to be inferred from the experience of her three lovers, while the dreadful nature of the mystery thus revealed can only be surmised from the fact that the very mention of it drove from her those who had loved her so passionately. Their subsequent fate was, in my opinion, the result of her vindictive remembrance of their desertion of her, and that they were forewarned of it at the time was shown by the words of both Reeves and Cowles. Above this, I can say nothing. I lay the facts soberly before the public as they came under my notice. I have never seen Miss Northcott since, nor do I wish to do so. If by the words I have written I can save any one human being from the snare of those bright eyes and that beautiful face, then I can lay down my pen with the assurance that my poor friend has not died altogether in vain.